the last snake in ireland

A STORY ABOUT ST. PATRICK

Sheila MacGill-Callahan   illustrated by Will Hillenbrand

HOLIDAY HOUSE/NEW YORK

For Maria Fernandez and Justin Callahan,
a wedding present
S. M-C.

For John and Kate
W. H.

EVERYONE KNOWS THAT PATRICK sent the snakes out of Ireland because they were so naughty folks were sick and tired of having them around. He'd tried for years to make them behave, but they just laughed at him. Then he found a gang of them teasing his old lame dog, Finbar, and he lost his temper.

Twined around a bush in a grassy hollow was the biggest, oldest, sneakiest snake in all of Ireland.

"Why aren't you off with the others?" asked Patrick.

"I didn't want to go. That ocean is a nasty, cold sort of place for an old gentleman like me, so I just stuffed some leaves in my ears so I couldn't hear your bell. I like it here at home."

Patrick knew it would do no good to ring his bell again; he'd used up all its snake magic.

"Won't you be lonely?" he asked.

The snake gave Patrick a scornful hiss and slid away.

Whenever Patrick went out, the snake was waiting. If he walked in the forest, the snake leaned down from a branch to tap him on the head.

When he talked with his friends in the evening, the snake looked in at the window. If he sat in the doorway with a mug of buttermilk, the snake oozed up to take a swig.

Patrick even found him under the quilt on his bed.

Patrick thought and thought about what to do. It wouldn't be sporting to give the miserable creature no chance at all. Finally, he came up with a plan. He made a box of rare wood and lined it with wool. On the lid he carved the snake's picture painted as red as the Red Hound of Ulster. He fitted each side of the box with an iron bolt that would slide home when the lid closed. Then he waited for summer to end.

On the first chilly day of autumn, Patrick made his way to the snake's den by Lough Finn. The snake was not happy to see him. He really didn't like Patrick very much. He showed his fangs.

"What do you want? Don't you know it's time for me to go to sleep until spring?" he hissed.

"I've been thinking about that," said Patrick, "and I've worried about you all alone in that cold hole with the snow falling down and the ice filling in your front and back doors. Just to show there are no hard feelings, I've made you a fine, warm house where you can lie snug all winter. You have to think about tomorrow."

"Got my own house," the snake said grumpily. He was very sleepy. "As far as I'm concerned, tomorrow is April First, because that's when I plan to wake up."

"There's no call for you to be so touchy. I'll just leave your fine new house here by the edge of the lough in case you want to look it over." If there was one thing Patrick was sure of, it was that snakes are very curious creatures.

He left the box on the shore and hid behind a bush.

It wasn't long before the snake's head popped out of the hole. He looked all around. When he was sure Patrick was nowhere around, he went to inspect the box.

"My, my," he muttered. "For sure that's the handsomest box ever made in Ireland." He wanted it more than anything he had ever seen, but he didn't trust the four iron bolts. Maybe, he thought, I could pull the box deep into my hole so no one can lock it while I'm inside. First, I'd better make sure that it fits.

He crawled in onto the fine wool cushion and he fitted exactly. He was so comfortable that he would have gone to sleep then and there if Patrick hadn't popped out from behind the bush.

"How do you like your new house?"

Wirra, wirra, I'm undone entirely, thought the snake. Quick as a wink he swelled himself up until he was spilling over the sides. "See, it's much too small. But it was a kindly thought and I thank you."

"Now, now," crooned Patrick, who was standing over the box. "I'm sure that if you pull yourself in a little you'll find it a fine fit."

Like lightning he moved to slam the lid, but the snake was even faster. He erupted in a fiery streak and made for the hills, with Patrick rushing after, carrying the box and roaring at the top of his lungs.

The snake slithered up one side and down the other of the Blue Stack Mountains. With the strength of his anger upon him, Patrick pushed the mountains open, forming the Long Glen of Hunting, which you can see to this day, and lay in wait on the other side.

The snake passed him too quickly to be caught and plunged into Lough Erne with Patrick swimming behind. They flashed through the Glens of Antrim and tip-tap-tipped across the Giants' Causeway where, at last, they were halted by the sea.

"I've got you now, my sly one," Patrick crooned as he lowered the box, hoping the snake would jump in.

And the snake was about ready to give up, when an eagle swooped down and caught him in her talons.

"Help me, Patrick! Help!" he yelled.

Now, it's true that Patrick wanted to get rid of the snake, but not this way. It was his snake and he wanted the victory to be his victory. He jumped into a coracle beached upon the shore, laid the box at his side, and paddled after the bird.

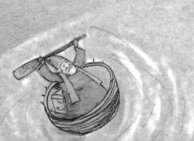

She headed over the Isle of Mull and up the Firth of Lorne, until she came to her aerie above Loch Ness, where the hungriest eaglets in all of Scotland waited for their dinner.

The eagle was brave, the eagle was clever, but she was no match for Patrick. With one jump he leaped from the coracle to the nest and lifted her over his head. Her beak fell open and the snake fell into the open box below. The lid snapped shut and the bolts slid into place.

Patrick jumped down, overturning the boat, and spilled the box overboard.

"Let me out!" the snake cried. "Let me out and back to Ireland. I promise I'll be good!"

"And so I will," Patrick crooned as he righted the coracle for his homeward journey, "but you'll have to wait until tomorrow."

Years later, when he was much closer to being a real saint, Patrick started to worry about how the snake was doing. He made the journey to the banks of Loch Ness. "I'm here," he shouted at the top of his lungs. "Tomorrow has finally come."

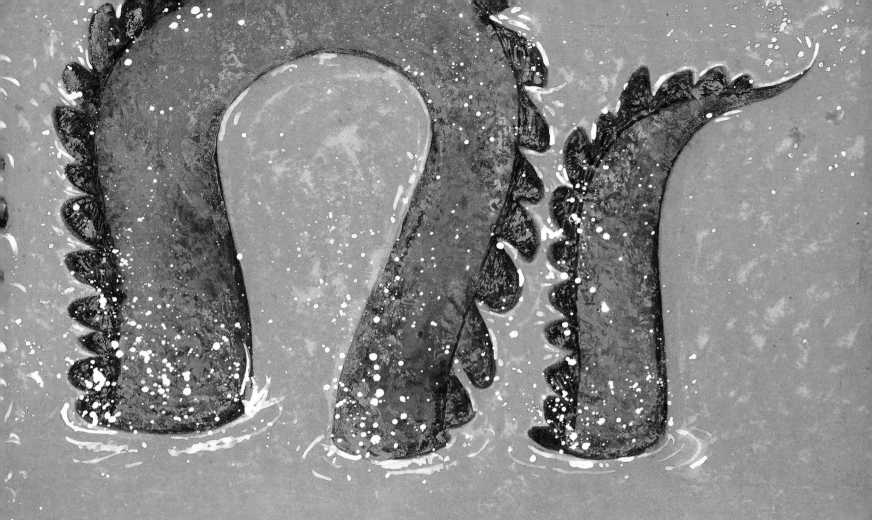

There was a troubling of the water as the surface was broken by huge red coils. Patrick jumped back in alarm as a face the size of a house loomed above him, its forked tongue flickering in and out. It was his old enemy, the snake.

"S-s-so," he hissed, "it's tomorrow, is it? You took your time."

Patrick plucked up his courage, "But I'm here, and you don't seem to have done too badly."

"Small thanks to you. As soon as I hit the water I started to grow and I never stopped. There's a good magic for snakes in this Loch. Your puny box broke into little pieces with the pressure."

He grinned. "I like it here. They call me the Loch Ness Monster."

AUTHOR'S NOTE: Scholarly works give short shrift to the legend of
St. Patrick and the snakes. Snakes and reptiles are not native to Ireland.
The poor creatures didn't make it across the land bridge from England before
the sea rose and divided the two islands at the end of the last Ice Age.

However the story started, it is the one thing that everybody knows about
Ireland's patron saint. The oldest account I have found is *The Life and Acts
of St. Patrick* by Jocelin, a compendium of wonders. This was first published
at Louvain, and there are copies there and at Trinity College, Dublin.
The original twelfth century manuscript is at the Irish College in Rome.
The translation I was fortunate enough to find was published by
P. J. Kennedy, New York, 1883 (7th Ed.).

The Loch Ness Monster has no such venerable history. In April 1933
a motorist driving by the loch reported seeing a strange creature in the water.
Subsequent sightings were claimed of a snake-like creature about thirty feet
in length with flippers.

Investigations have never proved or disproved the creature's existence,
but the passage of more than fifty years has been sufficient to build a
substantial legend. I took a storyteller's liberty and combined the tales.

(Both lough and loch mean lake, but the first is used in Ireland, and the
latter in Scotland.)

ILLUSTRATOR'S NOTE: My last name,
Hillenbrand, will never sound Irish, not even on
St. Patrick's Day. However, Irish blood has flowed
down to me from my mother's side of the family. My
great-great grandparents were both born in Ireland.
James Miller emigrated when he was only thirteen
years old in 1850. Eliza Shorten came from County
Cork near the twin villages of Enniskeen and
Ballineen. James and Eliza were married in
Cincinnati in 1857. Together they had four children:
Elizabeth, William, George, and Nellie. Eliza told her
children of her home and family across the Atlantic.
She would also have told them legends of the
patron saint of the Emerald Isle, Patrick. It is in that
tradition of storytelling that I made the pictures for
this book. Now I can help pass this story along to
others with Irish-sounding, and not so Irish-sounding,
last names.

Many thanks to Bill and Jane Graver, who took
the time to research and compile this family history.

Text copyright © 1999 by Sheila MacGill-Callahan
Illustrations copyright © 1999 by Will Hillenbrand
All rights reserved
Printed in the United States of America

Library of Congress Cataloging-in-Publication Data
MacGill-Callahan, Sheila.
The last snake in Ireland: a story about St. Patrick/ by Sheila MacGill-Callahan;
illustrated by Will Hillenbrand. — 1st ed.
p.   cm.
Summary: Before he becomes a saint, Patrick drives all the snakes but
one out of Ireland and that last one ends up in Scotland's Loch Ness.
ISBN 0-8234-1425-6
1. Patrick, Saint, 373?-463?–Legends.
[1. Patrick, Saint, 373?-463?–Legends. 2. Folklore–Ireland.] I. Hillenbrand, Will, ill.
II. Title.
PZ8. 1.M1715Las 1999
270.2'092—dc21

98-33504
CIP AC
ISBN 0-8234-1555-4 (pbk.)

The artwork for this book was done on vellum painted on both sides
with a mixture of media including oil pastel, egg tempera, watercolor, and water soluble artist crayons,
with a combination of 2b, 6b, and 9b woodless pencils.

The display type is set in Kells; the body text is Bodoni Book.